Happy READING!

Frank Fiorello

With love and gratitude for my wife Susan,
to my bighead children with wonderment,
and a great big thanks to the curious cats
who have graced our pumpkin patch.
Frankendad

PUMPKIN PATCH

CATS

Written & Illustrated by
Frank Fiorello

10 9 8 7 6 5 4 3 2

Library of Congress
Catalog Card Number: 96 96485

Paperback ISBN: 0-9646300-1-X

ot so long ago. . .

Deep in the land of orange,

Near
the famous
Caledonia
pumpkin
tree,

And by the old harvest barn,

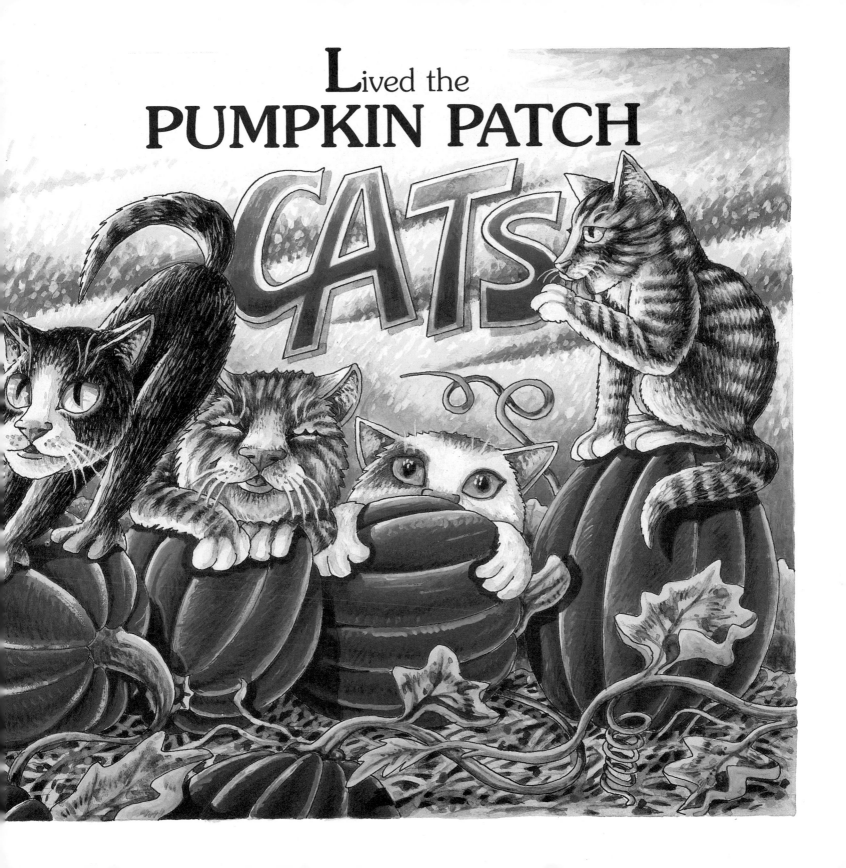

These
were no
ordinary
cats

Besides being barn yard mousers,

And friends to the patch animals,

They were also known in the local cat community as HALLOWEEN CATS

There was Chewey, the wise cat, who had survived years living at the patch.

Next was Caramel, the gentle cat, who liked to curl up on warm autumn afternoons.

Tiger Stripes was admired for her beautiful stripes and was nicknamed T.S.

Black Cat arrived one day, unannounced, knowing he had a home for autumn. It seems the colors orange and black mix well in October.

Next was
Fat Cat, who had
a head too large
for his body.

Joya was the happy cat, always jumping as if scared out of her skin.

Finally, there
was Baby Cat,
who was the
pumpkin of
everyone's eye.

Now, these Pumpkin Patch cats enjoyed the fall. . . but most of all they loved Halloween.

It was on Halloween night that the cat parade took place and Pumpkin Patch cats dreamed of leading the parade.

Each cat had to wear a costume. The best costume chosen by Patches, the loft scarecrow, would lead the parade.

So, on Halloween night, after the last customer left the old harvest barn, cats would come out to pick their costumes.

Chewey Cat became

T.S.
became

MUMMY
CAT

Black Cat
saw himself
as a

PIRATE

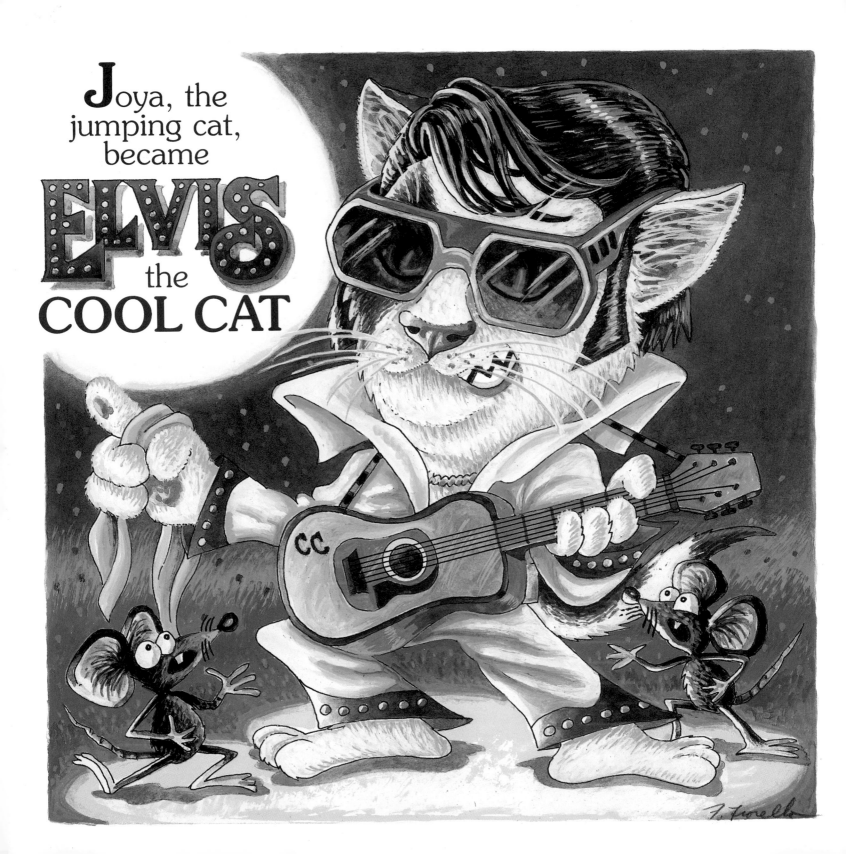

Joya, the jumping cat, became **ELVIS** the **COOL CAT**

And Baby Cat dressed up as
BABY CAT

All the cats in costume lined up for judging.

Patches, the loft scarecrow, chose the cat who would lead the parade

and he chose. . .

Caramel, the cowgirl cat!

Now all is ready for Halloween.

Kids are out trick or treating.

And the **PUMPKIN PATCH**

Happy Halloween from the PUMPKIN PATCH